REAPER BLISS

A Cornwall and Redfern Mystery

Book 4.5, A Bliss & Neil Halloween Short

Gloria Ferris

Table of Contents

DEDICATION

THIS FUN STORY IS FOR all you ghoulies and ghosties who love Halloween and/or Samhain.

"The spirits laugh and whisper,
Halloween has turned to Samhain."

Author: Me

Samhain (British & Canadian pronunciation *Sown*
American pronunciation **Saa** *wn*)

CHAPTER 1

BALANCING AN EXTRA-large take-out pumpkin spice coffee in one hand and carrying two grocery bags in the other, I kicked the door until Neil opened it.

He relieved me of the bags, chiding me for not texting him from the driveway to help. "No need for you to carry heavy bags. That's what husbands are for."

I let that one go. I'd shopped, set the items on the conveyer belt, bagged them myself, then moved them from cart to the back seat of my vehicle. Carrying the bags another twenty metres into the kitchen wasn't such a big deal as to require the assistance of a man.

Neil pawed through the bags, frowning as he placed each item on the table. "Pumpkin spice tea, pumpkin spice coffee pods, pumpkin spice cake. Shall I put these with the pumpkin spice candles and the pumpkin spice air freshener you put in both bathrooms?"

"Silly man. These are food items." I picked up the cakes and the pumpkin spice tarts he hadn't noticed. "These go in the freezer for later. The tea and coffee pods can go on the top shelf with the rest of my collection."

"You mean your hoard?"

"Now, don't be like that. This flavour is only available until the end of the month, which is today. My *hoard* has to last until next October." I sniffed his just-showered skin. "You didn't use the pumpkin spice body wash I bought for you. Don't you like it?" I tried not to smirk. I bought the body wash as a joke. I used it myself. I smelled like Halloween, my favourite holiday.

He shoved the non-perishables on the top shelf of my staples cupboard, which was nice of him considering he hated anything pumpkin spice. I wrapped the cakes and tarts in protective baggies and stowed them in the upright freezer. I lit a pumpkin spice-scented candle and placed it on the counter.

"What's for dinner?" He scanned the kitchen with his navy-blue eyes. "It's your turn, but I'll start the barbecue if you want."

"Not necessary, my gorgeous Viking. Can't you smell anything at all? The crock pot is filled with delicious chicken stew. A healthy salad is waiting in the fridge with the dressing I made this morning." I slurped at my take-out cup. Cold. I put it in the microwave to re-heat.

"Don't call me that, and all I can smell is that weird spice. Real pumpkins don't smell like anything much. What can I do to help?"

"Sit at the island and talk to me. Starting with, why aren't you patrolling the streets with your officers, harassing kids who just want to have fun on Halloween." I eyed his tight black tee shirt and form-fitting black jeans. "Wear your black leather jacket and you'll blend in with the night creatures."

"I'm going out around eight o'clock to relieve Margo. She wants to take her kids to a Halloween party."

"How's that for timing? I'm going to the greenhouse at the same time. Open house, with a spooky theme. I'm the Grim

Reaper."

His turn to look me up and down. "I thought the Grim Reaper would be taller, not five-foot-nothing."

"I'm five-two and sick of reminding you. Anyway, listen to this. I have to stand on a rock in the tropical greenhouse, wearing a hooded robe and waving a scythe at the visitors."

"At least I won't have to arrest my own wife for egging windows and turning over outhouses. If you can find an outhouse."

I winked at him. "The greenhouse closes at ten o'clock. After that, you'll never find me, copper."

As well as running a residential and commercial cleaning business, I worked 15 hours a week at the Belcourt Nursery as a collection agent. Take my word for it, Anything-for-a-Buck Bliss Moonbeam Cornwall didn't make a spectacle of herself as an underworld superhero unless she was paid extra, and I mean *very* extra.

My husband of two months, Neil Redfern, was the Chief of Police for Lockport, a small town on the shores of Lake Huron. We met a year and a half ago over a couple of dead bodies. We'd fallen in lust, then love, broke up more than once, and decided we worked better together than apart. The entire populace was relieved when we got married and moved outside the confines of the town limits. Good for us, too. We were able to loudly discuss our issues without nosy neighbours hanging off their back decks.

Now, here we were, in our first house located far too close to the water on Seahorse Bay. But, you know, we make sacrifices for the one we love. We were both 32 and he made increasingly-frequent comments about me laying a couple of eggs he could fertilize. He didn't put it quite like that, but that's how I took it. I was thinking about it.

He set the table while I tossed the salad and thought about the robe I had to wear. It was too long for me and I couldn't run if I tried. Standing on a rock beside the stream running through a trough carved into the tiled floor of the tropical greenhouse wasn't high up on my bucket list. The stream was filled with water plants and reptiles, mostly turtles and frogs, but I wouldn't put it past Chesley Belcourt to sneak in a couple of snakes for the Halloween gala. I focused on the money and that calmed me somewhat. It was only for a few hours. I could do it.

I finished my flavoured coffee and sat down again while Neil ate a second helping of the stew. "Do you want a piece of cake for dessert?"

He blew out my scented candle and waved away the fragrant smoke, grimacing like he smelled sulphur fumes from Hades. "If it's pumpkin spice, no."

"Fine. You get nothing." I ate both pieces, then made another coffee.

While he cleared the dinner dishes, I watched the way the overhead light glimmered off his blond hair. My gaze swept down the muscles of his back to his calves and thighs. I never tired of the sight.

"Quit staring at my ass," he said without turning around.

"You stare at mine."

"True enough. Carry on, then. We'll take my Jeep. I'll drop you off at the greenhouse and pick you up at ten."

"No need. I'm attending a Samhain ceremony with the local Wiccans after the greenhouse gig. I'll drive myself."

He eyed me suspiciously. "Will this ceremony take place in a cemetery?"

"Best you don't think too hard about that."

CHAPTER 2

IN THE STAFF WASHROOM, I removed my clothes — except underwear — before donning the hooded robe. Chesley ordered me not to show my face which I fully understood. I'm pretty cute, and a glimpse of my features would ruin the terror he wished to inflict on the public.

Well, screw him. What use was a cute reaper? I used black lipstick on my mouth and smeared more around my eyes and drew a beard around my chin line.

I shimmied in front of the mirror, singing, "I'm too sexy for my robe."

A fist hammered on the door and Chesley bellowed. "Move it, Bliss. It's almost showtime."

I lifted the hem of the robe to avoid tripping and dragged the six-foot scythe behind me to the tropical section of the Belcourt Nursery complex.

The scythe was plastic and wouldn't scare an infant, let alone the world-weary teenagers who were bound to drop a can of soup in the donation box and slouch through our terrifying Halloween display. I knew a farmer who had a real scythe in his barn and offered to loan it to me, but Chesley nixed the idea.

A few skeletons hung from the taller trees, and carved pumpkins lit from within by strings of orange or white lights lay scattered about the floor. A rocking chair held a dummy of a blood-soaked axe-murderer, a realistic-looking axe in hand. The display was set on a timer, so every five minutes, the dummy's arm rose and brandished the axe while the rocker rocked and the dummy moaned. It might startle a newborn, but that's it.

Plastic cauldrons of candy were strewn throughout the room, every one beyond my reach. I should have filled my underwear with candy before stepping onto my perch. The robe didn't have pockets.

The real stars of the show were the masses of black-blossomed flowers in orange pots grouped at the entrance to the greenhouse and lining the path along the stream — orchids, calla lilies, succulents, carnations, and a host of other exotic flowers I couldn't name. White lilies in black pots were artistically situated among the black flowers for contrast. They were all for sale.

Chesley's mum, Ivy Belcourt, permitted him to hold the Halloween extravaganza and allow the public to tramp through the greenhouse after he assured her that the revenue from the rare black flowers would more than offset paying me twice my usual hourly rate, not to mention the hours the greenhouse workers put in keeping the delicate blooms alive until October 31. I mustn't forget to mention the black butterflies that Chesley hatched from pupae to flit amongst the flowers. I'd seen the invoices for the pupae — they didn't originate from the Northern Hemisphere and cost more than silver per gram.

Ivy insisted on an entrance fee — a cash donation to the Lockport food bank as well as a food item. This afternoon, she'd fixed her only son with a hard eye and warned him that this was a trial run. If the Halloween event lost money, no more artsy-fartsy displays. Her words. Therefore, the plants better sell.

Fifteen minutes until the doors opened. We'd be lucky to get a dozen customers. I stabilized myself on my rock, feet bare for traction and placed wide apart, the useless scythe planted in front like a third leg. Two hours. Piece of cake.

I took a sip from my travel cup of pumpkin-spice coffee and pulled the hood over my face. I looked across at my fellow Reaper.

"Hey, Ciera," I called. "I can see your blonde braid hanging out."

She tucked the hair inside her hood and gave me a thumb's up.

"How come you get to stand on level ground, while I'm teetering on this rock?"

Chesley had positioned Ciera near the wooden bridge over the stream. She was Chesley's true love which is why she was safe from plunging into the water and risking a possible concussion or snake bite. I wanted her to admit to favouritism.

"I'm not good with heights, Bliss. If you feel the least bit dizzy, come right down."

And, stand near the water filled with reptiles? Yup, that would happen. "I'm good here. Maybe ..."

Chesley entered the greenhouse, having changed into his costume. "Alright, it's exactly 8 p.m. Mum is manning the outer doors, taking money and donations. Bliss, stop rocking back and forth and stand still until it's time to scare the kids."

"Trick or treat, smell my feet," I responded.

"Real mature." To Ciera, he said, "You look absolutely stunning, my love."

Stunning? Clad in a reaper robe with no skin or hair showing? Okay then, I was stunning as well.

But, I had to know. "Ches, are you supposed to be Ichabod Crane? I don't think he wore a red jacket and white pants."

I was kind enough not to mention he looked like the Sleepy Hollow hero on a good day — tall, lanky, sticky-out ears, shoulder-length hair pulled back in a skimpy ponytail.

"I'm wearing a British officer's red dress jacket and the traditional white trousers, as I'm sure you can see." He pulled an object from behind his back. "Here's my bicornuate hat."

I looked over at Ciera, but her face was hidden in the folds of her hood. I turned back to Chesley and took a wild stab. "You're an officer in the War of 1812?"

"Exactly. My great-great-grandfather fought in that war. Then he stayed here, married a settler, and that's why we're Canadian."

"Got it." Although there had to be a few more 'greats' in there. "Put your bicorn on. Here come the invading masses of Halloween crazies."

He jumped up and grabbed the cup from my hand.

"Hey!"

"Reapers don't drink coffee."

CHAPTER 3

HUGE YAWN. PARENTS herded their little ones through the tropical paradise and, to my surprise, most left with a plant or two. That was a shocker – the plants, including the white lilies, were mostly alien to these shores and wouldn't last a week without specialized care. Care which Chesley explained in depth to the bored customers before they left, and included written instructions. They cost thirty-four-ninety-five each which goes to show, people will buy anything if it looks exotic.

While Chesley educated the new black flower owners, the kids ran rampant through the forest of tropical trees and grabbed candy from the cauldrons.

One kid passed me with a fistful of chocolate bars. I pulled back my hood to make myself heard. "Psst. Hey, little girl, can you hand me a couple of those?"

She had to be at least seven years old, so I don't know why she let out such a loud screech. I pulled the hood back over my face and stood still as a statue while the little diva ran to her parents and pointed back at me. At that moment, the axe murderer did his thing, raising his bloody hatchet and moaning. That kid should never have been brought to a Halloween display, that's all I have to say. The family left with two dark plants each, with the kid howling and dropping candy in her wake.

Only twenty minutes had passed. Despite my prediction of a no-show event, the place filled up. Chesley's grin reached from ear to ear as the plants steadily exited. Most customers left with a bonus – a black butterfly or two nestled in their hair.

I'd learned my lesson. When a pink-cheeked cherub reached over to pick a flower, I kept my hood in place and intoned, "Pluck a dark blossom, and Death shall follow you home."

That kid had a meltdown and was carried out by his father with the mom trailing behind balancing three dark flowers. Bet the kid would keep his hands to himself from now on.

The expected teens came. They sneered, they stuffed their pockets with candy. They didn't wear costumes other than the usual punk rocker regalia which I didn't recognize. I slid back my hood and watched them closely. They glanced at me, snickered, and walked by. Except for one.

She pursed her black lips. "You're not scary. Nice flowers, though. Are they free? I think I'll take this one."

Half expecting I'd have to jump down and wrestle one of Chesley's Gothic Black Spider Mums from her grasp, I caught her eye and said, "We are born of Chaos, and to Chaos we shall return. Especially, if we believe anything in life is free."

"Whatever." She kicked over a white lily and scampered after her friends who stood in front of the axe murderer, nudging each other and laughing.

I nearly lost my footing on the rock when the dummy jumped to his feet and flourished the axe at the teenagers, roaring in a guttural voice, "Kill, kill, die."

They ran, he gave chase, his tattered, bloody bits of

clothing trailing behind. Right past me they raced, towards the bridge. My fellow Reaper stepped out of their way into the water. By this time, I clued in the "dummy" was one of the greenhouse workers, co-opted to act as murderous dead guy. Pretty sure the axe wasn't a plastic prop after all. I cheered him on, swinging my scythe in the air.

The girls screamed, as well as some of the boys. They ran by my rock again. Chesley opened the door and they ran through, waving off the black butterflies dive-bombing them.

Ivy wouldn't be happy. She was adamant that foreign insects not escape the greenhouse and mingle with the locals. Since it was the end of October with snow predicted any day, native butterflies had long departed for the south, so these poor things would freeze before their human hosts got them home. Along with the dark plants. Not my problem.

My problem was the rock. For the past twenty minutes, the heat and humidity of the greenhouse caused me to sweat under the heavy fabric of the robe. I could deal with that. But, my sweaty bare soles slid ever closer to the downward slope of the rock. No matter how far apart I planted my feet, the faster I slid. I'd soon be straddling the rock. The plastic scythe bent and threatened to snap in two. The primeval eyes of turtles and frogs broke the surface of the stream, watching, waiting for me. When I died, I'd haunt Chesley until *he* died, then I'd ...

Screw this. I sat down, stretching out my legs, arranging the folds of the robe to hide my unmentionables from phone cameras. Feeling the black makeup running down my cheeks and throat, I threw back the hood and waved at a family with three tots. Two of them broke into extreme blubbering which should make Chesley happy, as terror for the multitudes was his goal for the night. The axe murderer chased off any teenagers who lingered too long or snatched too much candy.

Two cops came in, the young ones Neil recently hired right out of Police College. Their names escaped me. I did my best not to giggle. They hadn't been on the job long enough to walk normally in a non-threatening situation. Hands on belt, they swaggered close to Chesley.

"Who you supposed to be?" The taller one asked. He sported a bald fade haircut, but the stylist had left the hair on top too long. He looked like a brown-crested cockatoo.

"A British officer from the War of 1812. My ancestor," Chesley replied, straightening his shoulders and re-positioning his bicornuate hat.

"Cool," the second cop said. His head sprouted red fuzz, almost ready for another once-over with the razor.

"Hey. Stan and Ollie," I called. "Help yourselves to some candy, and bring a couple chocolate bars to me, please."

"You're supposed to be a menacing underworld reaper, not filling your face with chocolate," Chesley barked. He tried to be my boss but, as anyone will tell you, he lost that battle long ago.

"My name is Officer Tristan McNally, and this is Officer Ben Minor." He scooped up an entire kettle and brought it over to me.

I grabbed a half dozen of the mini bars. "Thanks. Fill your pockets. We're almost done here." Wishful thinking. We had at least another hour of this insanity.

"Well, aren't you a delicious little snack yourself?" Tristan drawled, while Ben pulled at his arm. Tristan shrugged him off. I didn't say anything.

"How about some one-on-one trick or treating later?"

Tristan set his cap on his head and looked invitingly at me. "I can see that under the black makeup, you're sizzling hot. I can give you some treats you won't soon forget."

I shot my left hand from under my Reaper cuff and contemplated the black nail polish and my black rhodium wedding ring set with black diamonds. No boring white diamond engagement ring and plain platinum band for me.

"So, how married are you? Up for some treats?" Tristan asked, eyeing the ring.

"You idiot. That's the Chief's wife. Word is, he still likes her." Ben rammed his knuckles into Tristan's bicep.

"Shit. Why didn't you tell me?" He took a step back from my rock. "I'm really sorry, Mrs. Redfern. Just a joke."

Please don't tell your husband, I beg of you, was his unspoken plea.

"Call me Bliss. I'll let it go this time, but if I hear of you hitting on another woman while in uniform, or off duty for that matter, I'll ensure you're downgraded to meter boy. I have great influence with your boss. He *really, really* likes me."

Tristan thrust another half dozen chocolate bars at me, then turned and beat feet for the exit. Ben sent me an apologetic look before following his friend.

The next hour passed faster than I anticipated and turned out to be more fun than I expected. Lots of little kids would have nightmares for a few years.

We actually ran over the two hours before fright night at the greenhouse ended. I made a note of the exact time the last visitor left. I didn't work for free.

CHAPTER 4

WHILE CHESLEY UNWOUND the axe man from his bloody bandages — he turned out to be Alistair McKnight, one of our fulltime workers — Ciera and I changed in the staff bathroom. She did, anyway, looking angelic in a white robe over white, full-length skirt and heavy knit white sweater.

After scrubbing my face clean, I put my jeans and sweatshirt on, then replaced the black Reaper robe. Ciera gave me a side-eye, but didn't remark on my lack of Wiccan white.

Chesley had lots to say about it, though.

"We're attending a celebration with the spirits of the departed. White attire is appropriate. Black is not. You might frighten them away if they see a Reaper. How do you think they got to the afterlife?"

"Uh, their souls floated through a tunnel to the other side where they were greeted by long-dead loved ones and beloved pets. Reaper shit is just a myth. I'm sure the souls don't care what colour robes we wear. Anyway, do you really expect spirits to pop up and party with you?"

Ciera was the Wiccan priestess or chieftain, or whatever the head of the group of nature worshippers called herself. Chesley knew marginally more about the Wiccan religion than me, but a whole lot less than Ciera. "She'll be okay, sweetie,"

Ciera told her beloved. "I'm sure the spirits will judge us on our intentions, not the colour of our robes."

Alarm bells rang in my head. "Wait a minute, here. We're going to a cemetery, right? This is all for fun, right?"

Ciera patted my arm. "On November 1st, beginning at midnight October 31st, the veil between worlds thins to the point where departed souls may cross through and visit with us for a few minutes or hours if they choose. We honour them with a bonfire and set out food and mead as symbols of our welcome."

"Sort of like milk and Christmas cookies for Santa Claus, right? Because Santa is a myth and nobody expects him to appear in the middle of their fireplace on Christmas Eve. So, all this is just a fun party on Halloween night, right? We get to eat the food and drink the mead. I made a taco dip to share with the others."

Ciera fastened her robe over her ample chest. "Samhain is not a myth. There are many accounts of spirits manifesting on this night in bygone times. We're going to celebrate in a cemetery because that might give us the best chance of welcoming actual spirits into our gathering."

Nobody loves cemeteries more than I do. One of my jobs for the town of Lockport is routinely inspecting the many active and abandoned cemeteries and graveyards to ensure they hadn't in any way been desecrated. It's one of my favourite jobs. I love the beauty of the statuary, and the stories engraved on the epitaphs. Sometimes I talk to the residents.

When I was a teenager, I joined my posse in respectfully drinking toasts to the departed during the darkest of nights, usually in the summer. These days, I preferred the warmth of the sun as I walked among the dead. I never detected foreign energies or witnessed wisps of gossamer ectoplasm in any of the burial places I checked.

I asked Ciera, "Have you ever seen a spirit?" Maybe I should just go home to my husband and watch a couple of horror movies while we ate the tacos and dip.

"Not yet. The last couple of years we celebrated Samhain on a hilltop with the wind blowing through our hair and the trees whispering to us but …"

"The wind kept blowing out the fire. It started to snow." Chesley shivered and edged closer to Ciera.

"Did the trees whisper anything you could understand? Like, get the hell out of here before you burn the entire forest down."

"You're so silly, Bliss," Ciera said. "We're going to celebrate in a cemetery this year to be closer to the spirits. I hope one or two will sense our devotion to nature and our sincere wish to communicate. If not, we still honour their memories."

"We should get going soon," Chesley said. "The others will be gathering and waiting for us." He'd changed out of his ancestral costume into white, flowy pants and sweater. A white robe that matched Ciera's was fastened to his throat, the cowl, draped artfully at the back of his neck.

"How many in the flock this year?" I wondered aloud. If any spirits did cross over for a look-see on how far the world had devolved in their absence, they might be pissed to find a living person lounging on their tombstone.

"I expect about a dozen. Just the most devout," Ciera answered. "Some of our newer members are still somewhat skittish about the more spiritual aspects of our faith."

I had a thought. "Are you all going to get naked and jump over the fire?" Because I didn't want to see that and wouldn't trust myself not to take photos.

"It's usually too cold for that at Samhain," Chesley said. "Nothing but respect for the spirits." I virtually saw a halo form around his head. Hmmm.

I'm not a Wiccan, in case anyone is wondering. It just sounded like fun: cemetery, midnight, mead, food, bonfire. Substitute tequila for the mead, and you had my teenage years.

"Okay, here's the thing," I looked from one to the other. "I judge no religion as long as it doesn't subjugate others, especially women. But, I'm attending tonight as custodian of the cemetery. I will be there to protect the integrity of the site. I know neither of you will damage anything, but I may not know some of the others. At the first sign of danger to the graves, headstones, trees, or outbuildings, I will shut it down. Agreed?"

Chesley grumbled under his breath.

"What was that?" I whipped my head around and narrowed my eyes at him.

"Who made *you* boss of anything?" He enunciated every word clearly like I couldn't speak English.

"Now, Chesley, Bliss will be performing due diligence, and the spirits always recognize positive vibes. It may help them feel comfortable enough to come through."

I refrained from rolling my eyes. "I have a suggestion I'm sure you'll get behind, Chesley."

"And, what might that be? Make it snappy. We have to get the plants that require cooler temps back to their correct rooms before we leave." He forgot to take off his navy blue bicorn and it looked hilarious with his robe. I didn't mention it.

"That's the thing. These remaining plants? Let's take them to the cemetery and leave them on the graves as gifts for the departed. Perhaps their spirits will be more willing to pop around for a visit."

Ciera gave me a disapproving look. She knew me well enough to know I didn't believe in ghosts, even on Halloween or Samhain, whichever. I wasn't sure why she persisted in inviting me to her Wiccan services. I didn't even go to regular church.

Chesley, on the other hand, believed there could be no greater gifts than plants, especially black ones, for the dead. His eyes lit up and he gathered up the leftovers close to the door to the hallway. By morning, the poor things would be deader than the bones in the graves below them but, hey, they were bound for an early death anyway. Might as well make it a quick one.

All were doomed but at least I wouldn't have to help lug them back to the correct greenhouse. There was a limit to my good nature. I waved off a trio of black butterflies that tried to fly under my robes.

Before we left the greenhouse, I found the nearly full cup of pumpkin spice coffee Chesley snatched from me earlier and heated it in the microwave.

What a laugh. I just made myself boss of Samhain.

CHAPTER 5

WHEN CIERA FIRST APPROACHED me about taking part in the Samhain celebration and using a cemetery this year, I insisted on picking the location. Many burial spots, some of them very old, were too visible to the public. Even adults weren't above grabbing a group of their friends and scaring themselves silly with a hasty tour of a countryside cemetery. And the younger people, well, the less said the better, and I should know.

The location of Ciera's ceremony had to take place in an old cemetery most people didn't know about. I had the perfect place. It was definitely perfect for a trio of teenagers who discovered the cemetery fifteen years ago and never shared the location with friends.

The official name of the cemetery was Darkwood Burial Ground, but the name was impossible to read on the crumbling stone pillars at its entrance. Some of the oldest burials in the tri-county area could be found there. My friends and I came across the lost cemetery during our final year of high school and we spent many a Saturday night sharing a bottle of tequila in complete safety from the cops. I rediscovered it last summer during a job I performed for the crazy-ass mayor of Lockport. She wanted me to find and enumerate all the burial places within the township, official and unofficial.

Every name on every tombstone went on a list. It took me all summer, part-time, to finish the task since I had many other jobs including my cleaning business. It was only later I found out Her Royal Mayoress Glory Yates hoped I'd locate the grave of her great-grandfather, an English stonemason who settled in these parts over a hundred years ago. I never found him and Glory wasn't pleased with me. No matter; she wasn't pleased about much except her hot OPP boyfriend, but that's another story.

Back in the nineteen-oughts, Darkwood belonged to Arran-Elderslie Township, part of Lockport's area of municipal control. That section of township changed hands several times since then and it was now a no-man's land, with neither the Lockport Police Service nor the South Bruce Ontario Provincial Police Detachment claiming it. Therefore, still the best place to not get raided on Halloween night, or Samhain morning, whatever.

I kind of hated to show Chesley, Ciera, and the dozen other members of the coven, my repository of private teenage memories. I solved that by leading the cavalcade around the sideroads in circles before bumping down an overgrown path leading to the cemetery.

Chesley was in the second vehicle, with five or six others following. With no room to turn around, everyone would have to back out onto the sideroad.

"Where are we?" were the first words out of Chesley's mouth. "I didn't bring a flashlight."

Neither had most of the other celebrants. I mean, come on, did they think there'd be floodlights here at the edge of the civilized world? Fortunately, I'd borrowed Neil's police flashlight he kept at home. I thoughtfully left my Canadian Tire model in its place in case he needed to go outside for any reason before I got home.

The police-issue gizmo had flashers and maybe even a siren, but I didn't want to wake the dead. Hah, good one, me.

With the band of white-clad, grumbling citizens following in my wake, I entered the grounds of Darkwood, carrying a bowl of dip and a jumbo-sized bag of taco chips, with the flashlight under my arm.

"Follow me, dear deathlings, but don't touch the pillars," I called over my shoulder. "They might fall on you." I was having second thoughts about this place. I didn't know the co-ordinates if we needed an ambulance, and I was sure to be blamed.

CHAPTER 6

THE WICCANS STUMBLED through the gates, dragging armfuls of firewood, two collapsible tables, four pumpkins, and three boxes of paraphernalia that Ciera needed to organize her altar. She, at least, had brought a flashlight. Chesley handed each celebrant a couple of flower pots to carry in as well.

"Don't put anything down yet," I called over my shoulder. "We're going to set up over by the fence at the back of the cemetery. Keep walking."

Once we reached the overgrown path taken by funeral processions long ago, I set the super-sized flashlight on a tall tombstone for optimum light and took Ciera's from her. While she and the others prepped the altar and feast tables, I walked along the path for twenty yards or so and laid it atop another tall marker.

Adjacent to the path was the barbed-wire fence that separated the cemetery from a corn field. The farmer had seemingly forgotten to harvest this little corner of his property, for the dried corn stalks still towered high over our heads, leaning over the fence as though they didn't want to miss the show. *Children of the Corn* kind of creepy.

"You look like a gargoyle, perched on that tombstone. Why can't you dress in white like everyone else?" Chesley called to me, dragging a couple of coolers closer to the feast table.

"Because I'm the Grim Reaper, and I'm watching for anyone who comes through the Veil. Back they go."

"You shouldn't talk like that, Bliss." Ciera placed a pumpkin at each corner of the altar cloth to anchor it to the table. She tossed a couple of gourds into the middle. "We're hoping for a spirit to come through. Please don't scare them away if it happens."

I rolled my eyes and pulled the hood over my head. I didn't have the scythe but managed a selfie, hoping the tombstones behind me would show up in the photo and provide the appropriate spooky ambience.

Ciera tenderly unwrapped Hector, her ancestral skull. Usually, Hector reposed on the front desk in her Above and Below Shop, but she always took him to solstices and equinoxes, and the most fun pagan holiday – Samhain.

Ciera beckoned her followers closer and recited what sounded like a Wiccan sacred text. "From ancient times to modern day, Samhain marks the end of summer, and the end of the harvest season. It represents the beginning of winter, which has a direct connection to death. The Veil between the living and the dead thins at midnight, allowing the spirits to venture through to visit the living, if they so wish. Let us begin."

As the celebrants moved back and forth through the light, I recognized most of them and, good grief, some of these people were quite unexpected: Elise Boudreau, my cousin's motherly housekeeper; Ian Mueller, owner of the tattoo shop in town; Delia Melancourt, the town clerk — I waved at her; Ken Murrison, the owner of the Hemp Hollow trailer park I lived in for two years when my first marriage exploded — long story but ended well for me and badly for the Weasel (my ex). I managed some shots of most of them before Chesley noticed me.

"Bliss, can you please put the phone away? This is a private ceremony. Maybe make yourself useful and dispense the plants among the dearly departed."

"Sure, boss, I'll be glad to help out." I could have told him to shove it, since my work for him ended at ten o'clock. I was only here as a favour to Ciera and, okay, curiosity. I attended her last Summer Solstice ceremony and wanted to know if anything different happened. For them, I mean. I had wandered off and been shot at by an automatic rifle-wielding gun runner and been forced to hurl a live grenade at him. Neil has never fully recovered emotionally from nearly losing me, although he hid it well most days. That was the night I proposed to him. A near-death experience makes you understand what's important.

I digress. The weather during the Summer Solstice party — held in a different cemetery chosen by Ciera — was balmy, so the Wiccans decided to go skyclad, which is witch-talk for buck naked. Apparently, you feel closer to nature that way. Uh-uh, not me. That's when I wandered off into the cross-hairs of the certifiably-crazy weapons provider to gangs and criminals.

October 31st was decidedly frosty and I could have used a winter jacket under the robe, so little chance of skyclad Wiccans.

First, I turned on my phone flashlight and gathered up as many white lilies as I could hold. I used three fingers of one hand to hold the phone and ventured into the darkness.

Staying in the shadows, I distributed the leftover plants.

The full moon occurred three days ago, called Hunter's Moon, according to Ciera who kept her eye on these things. Hanging low in the sky was the Waning Gibbous moon, still bright but, unfortunately, out here in the depths of who-cared, a mist had risen, hiding the tops of the trees and everything farther than two feet in front of me. No visible moon or starlight, and the darkness swallowed the light from my phone.

The fog thickened perceptibly, but I had good recall of the cemetery, having spent so many Saturday nights kicking back with my two best buds, talking about how we were going to escape Lockport and start up a tech company, make millions before selling the company to Bill Gates for billions. Tequila shots were involved.

Chico was the only one who had any technical expertise and he owned the Canadian Tire franchise in town, married young, and had two or three kids, I couldn't remember. Fang ran a local construction company, married and became the father of five kids, maybe six by now. He didn't seem to know how to stop.

Other than four years of university in Toronto because my first husband was studying law and I thought back then we would remain in love forever, I'd stayed in Lockport except for the odd vacation since I met Neil. Chico, Fang and I were still friends, but our high school years were long ago and far away – fifteen years to be exact.

I remembered the location of all the child graves and made three trips back to the light for more plants until they all had a while lily on their sad little stones.

The Wiccans lit the bonfire and began to chant. Someone

had a bongo — probably bongs were involved, too — and they settled in to wait. It was after midnight, so any minute now the spirits would begin to arrive. What if we ran out of mead and cakes? Would there be a ghost riot?

The thought of mead spurred me onwards. I tossed black flowers hither and yon among the tombstones, dropping one on my foot when a tiny black butterfly shot out from the blooms of an orchid-like plant. "Flee, little butterfly," I told it. "But, you won't escape your fate."

I placed the last pot on a nearby grave topped with a Celtic cross and sat down on an adjoining table tomb to rub my sore foot. I might have broken a few bones ...

The stone under my butt grew frigid, and it was cold to start with. I shone my light on the inscription. I knew this guy. Thomas Warrick, 1802 to 1887. He was quite an age when he passed, especially for that generation. Because he had a nice flat surface, we spent a lot of time sitting on old Thomas.

My foot clanked against something that sounded like ... uh-oh, it couldn't be, not after all this time. I felt around on the ground and came up with an empty, dirt-encrusted tequila bottle. What were chances?

I brushed off the bottle and stuck it in my tote. I was an avid re-cycler.

My butt was a block of ice. I stood up and looked around the base of Thomas's tomb, finding three more empties. They joined their brother in my bag.

I looked down at the grave. "Um, sorry Thomas. We were dumb teenagers. I thought we cleaned everything up back then. Although, to you, it might seem like just yesterday."

Okay, I mentioned I talk to dead people in cemeteries. I do

it all the time during my inspections. Never at night, though. Spooky. And, I never expect spirits to pop out of their graves to talk back.

"Sorry again," I said. The marble under my light glowed faintly, then subsided into a darker shade of stone than it should be.

Imagination. I had too much of it. I turned and hop-limped back to the light and warmth of the fire, my bag clanking with the evidence of a misspent youth.

CHAPTER 7

THERE'S NOTHING QUITE like bongo drums to set my teeth on edge, but I accepted a plastic wine glass of mead and scooped up a few cakes. The taco chips and dip had mostly disappeared. The mead was made from fermented honey instead of grapes if I had my facts straight. I wasn't fussy. I pretty much liked anything fermented, except beer and sauerkraut. And kefir. The tiny, round cakes were sticky and full of seeds that lodged between my teeth, but I was hungry and ate three before remembering my bag was stuffed with candy from the greenhouse.

Stepping back into the shadows, I chose the base of a tall obelisk-type monument to rest on and opened a bag of jelly beans. The chill of the stone seeped through my robe, but not half as bad as old Thomas's. I crammed my mouth with candy and dared a glance toward his grave. A glowing aura of light illuminated his gravestone.

I blinked, and Darkwood became full of mist and shadows again. I couldn't distinguish Thomas's grave from any other. Hella imagination I had. I went for more mead.

The temperature rose dramatically this close to the fire. The flames shot higher as the men (naturally, they love fires) added more logs.

I nudged Chesley. "Did anyone bring a fire extinguisher?"

"Why?"

"Because the wind is blowing the flames towards the fence line, and the dried-out corn stalks are right up against it. It's been a dry fall, and if a spark ignites even one stalk, I don't ..."

"Calm down." Chesley reached into a duffle bag near his feet and pulled out a fire extinguisher. One of the tiniest I'd ever seen.

"Keep it handy. You're going to need it." And, a fat lot of good it would do in the ensuing conflagration.

I moved up next to Ciera who lay out more cakes and another bottle of mead. I poured myself a libation, just a small one. I had to drive home.

A half dozen of the Wiccans swayed in time to the bongo music, their white garments fluttering in the breeze which looked very cool but, I have to point out, sent the flames ever closer to the corn. The "music" hammered into my brain, and I wanted to put my foot through the drums.

"So, Ciera," I said. "Where are the spirits coming from? The graves? Where is this *veil* you speak of? Have you ever summoned a spirit?"

"Such a lot of questions, Bliss." She flipped her blonde plait over her shoulder and nibbled daintily on a seed cake. "Since we're in a cemetery, we hope one of the departed will come forth. The Veil is a metaphorical essence."

"So, the spirits aren't going to part a real curtain and dance through in time to the bongos. Have you actually seen a spirit?"

"I haven't, but if everyone is in a higher spiritual space, we may entice one to cross over and meet with us, even for a few seconds. So, if you'll excuse me, I'll meditate and focus on the far side of the Veil. One of these years, it will happen. Samhain is a magical night."

"Got it. I'll be over there if you need me."

If I had the brains of a bird, I'd have left right then and run for my life through Darkwood's crumbing pillars. Jumped into my Matrix and gone home to my blond husband and the safety of our bed. Unfortunately, none of these celebrants knew where they were or how to get back to Lockport. I was stuck with them. To cement my helplessness, six or seven vehicles were parked up against mine outside the gates. I'd be last out after everyone else backout onto the sideroad.

Thus, I stayed, and what followed became Lockport Halloween lore, or Samhain legend, depending on your beliefs.

CHAPTER 8

I LEANED AGAINST THE fence close to Chesley's extinguisher and kept an eye on the fire. Let's face it, I brought these people here and, if something bad happened, it would take a lot of lying on my part to distance myself from any responsibility.

I noticed Garnet Maybe, owner of the Golden Goddess Spa, speaking confidentially with Ciera, who nodded a few times, then clapped her hands for attention. Whatever happened to meditation? The bongos ceased, thank the Underworld.

"Excuse me, everyone. Garnet has made an excellent suggestion. Since it's become so warm hear the fire, I invite anyone who wishes, to dance skyclad around the perimeter. Perhaps our absolute connection with nature will encourage a spirit or two to visit with us."

And ... here we go. I should have known. If only I could, in all good conscience, leave this nature-lovers' festivity. At least the fire was too high and wild for them to leap over. Which they did during the Summer Solstice ceremony, letting the fire die down to embers, then jumping over them, body parts swinging. That's when I left and nearly died.

I concentrated on unwrapping a mini chocolate bar,

avoiding the unwrapping of the Wiccans. I declined Ciera's invitation to join them. Not because I'm ashamed of my body. Far from it. I get naked for Neil all the time and he's never complained. But, most of these people were business owners or members of town council, and one of my jobs was assistant to the mayor, performing all the face-to-face interactions she didn't want to engage in. Dodging them in future so I wouldn't remember them naked — and vice versa — wasn't an option.

The bongos started up again. Thomas's grave blazed in my peripheral vision. The fire lapped at the fence line. I checked the field for sparks and almost peed myself.

Two pairs of white eyes blazed from the cornfield. My heart tripped double time before reason prevailed. A coyote pair, drawn by the warmth and light from the fire. Coyotes were abundant in the Bruce County forests, and seeing their eyeshine in the headlights of my car when driving home at night was a common sight.

"Shoo." I hissed at them. The eyes turned in my direction, then back to the fire. This was as close as I planned to get to a couple of wild animals. I picked up a small fallen branch and tossed it at the fence. It narrowly missed the dance troupe but no one appeared to notice. Wow, if they were in a trance, they'd miss out on everything – coyotes, glowing tombstone, the appearance of spirits, should they choose to check on the hell the world had turned into since they died in the nineteenth century.

The stick had one effect. Two snouts poked through the fence and a snarl joined the bongo noise. Okay, no more teasing the coyotes.

Against my better judgement, I risked another glance at

Thomas's site. The gravestone shone even brighter — no natural reason I knew of for that. Which sight would be more apt to send the Wiccans into a fear frenzy — wild animals, or glowing graves? I better warn them.

Where should I look, though? The grown-ass Wiccans — some of them middle-aged and beyond — cavorted around the firepit, trying to encourage the long-departed to return for a short visit. Hell, if I wasn't mistaken, their wish was about to come true. Ciera stated quite emphatically that spirits came forth only if they wanted to. But, perhaps all this ritual gave Thomas no choice but to bust through the Veil, and others would pop out of their graves as well. In which case, they'd be pissed and, really, who wanted to face pissy spirits? Not me.

Some things should not be messed with. I stared at Thomas's grave, thinking the spot would return to normal darkness if it was watched — you know, creepy things can only sneak up on you if you turn your back and don't look.

My lips went numb and I dropped my glass of mead and a wrapper from a Snickers bar.

Unless I was crazy, or drunk — the latter being my preferred option — a faint outline of a man hovered over the area where Thomas's bones lay. I blinked, but the outline remained. I looked at the cornfield. The coyotes hadn't left. Turning my head back to Thomas, he was still there and growing larger.

I willed myself to believe that one of the Wiccans decided to play a joke on his friends. The chill in my bones didn't believe that. I wanted to screech and run through Darkwood's gates, into the forest filled with coyotes, wolves, bats and who the shit knew. I couldn't even do that. My legs wouldn't move and no sound left my paralyzed throat. What if the entire cemetery manifested?

I wrenched my gaze from Thomas and forced myself to look at the naked witches. I tried to pick out Ciera. Being honest here; people without their clothes are hard to distinguish from each other. Except males and females, it goes without saying. And, if they're holding hands and skipping in a circle, it's darn near impossible.

There she was. I recognized her thick, blonde plait of hair hanging down her back, kicking up her heels between two skinny men, one of whom had to be Chesley. They wore their shoes, good call on the rutted, stony path.

My ice-block legs barely held me up as I stood. Still couldn't speak, let alone scream. I had to present Ciera and her coven with a real live spirit and I didn't care what they planned to do with it. Maybe one dearly departed would be enough for them, and we could skedaddle before the rest showed up.

This was bad, very bad. I never believed in ghosts but, now, actually experiencing one, I could no longer deny their existence. After tonight, I'd be looking for them everywhere. How could I perform my cemetery inspections after this, even in broad daylight?

If I saw a ghost, these witches would, too. Shared trauma had to be better than me seeing a ghost by myself. Who would believe us? We'd have to start a support group for survivors of spirit sightings. My stomach roiled. I shouldn't have eaten so much chocolate.

Waiting for Ciera to circle around closer to me so I could grab her and point, I heard feet crunching through the dead leaves, stopping just outside the flame-light. Two faceless forms wavered, screened by the billowing smoke. Spirits shouldn't make noise when they walk.

I slipped behind the obelisk and pulled the hood tightly around my face. I used to love Halloween.

CHAPTER 9

WHAT HORROR WAS THIS, now? Two uniformed cops drifted into view, jackets open to allow their fingers to hook over their belts. Rookies and, as they neared the firelight, their shoulder flashings identified them as Lockport Police Service members. That was good. OPP cops would arrest the entire bunch of us but I had a great deal of influence with the LPS. Not that Neil wouldn't spend the next sixty years citing this night as an example of the bad judgement I exhibited every time I left the house.

I changed my mind about their affiliation being a good thing when I caught a glimpse of the faces under the caps. Tristan and Ben. I stepped out from behind the tombstone.

Tristan smirked at me. "Betcha the boss doesn't know his wife is hanging out in a cemetery with a group of naked people."

"Betcha didn't know it's perfectly legal to be naked in a cemetery," I told him, without a clue if that was true but betting these two newbies wouldn't know either. "You're interrupting a religious event. That's against the law." Maybe.

"Come on, Tris," said his buddy, pulling on his arm. "Let's get out of this place."

"Yeah, beat it, Tris. This is a private affair. Why were you following us, anyway?" No way they found us by chance.

"Eight vehicles parading through town on Halloween night?" Tris sneered. "Not suspicious at all."

Slow learner, this boy. I spread out my arms. "Go ahead, Take my photo. Show it to your boss. I double-dog-dare you."

"I can take photos of the rest of these religious nutters. He won't like that."

I made a show of looking around at the Wiccans. "Uh, go ahead, Einstein."

To a man — and woman — every member of the coven was decently clad in a white robe reaching the ground. Piles of underwear, sweaters, and pants lay scattered on the ground but, again, not illegal.

"Nothing to see here, fellas."

I almost wanted Neil to be informed of the proceedings, including photos of the celebrants. He'd be furious to see some of the influential citizens of Lockport harassed by his two most junior rookies. Or one. I'd make sure Neil knew that Ben was not a participant in this ridiculous show of authority.

I glanced left toward Thomas's grave. Still there. If anything, his silhouette was sharper than before within its cocoon of fog. Why hadn't anyone else noticed it. On my right side, the coyote snouts poked through the fence and two sets of white eyes fixated on the repast table. Was everyone here so concerned with the baby cops they didn't see the real dangers?

Would a ghost or wild animals be more likely to send the cops on their way? One good thing about the two uninvited wingnuts — their arrival had broken the spell paralyzing my voice and body.

I took a step closer to Ciera and pointed at Thomas. "Our

first guest just arrived." I hoped with every fibre of my being that she would see him too. No one wants to be the only person in a cemetery to see a spirit.

I needn't have worried. The collective gasp, and a few shrieks confirmed that Thomas's essence was visible to all.

Two guns shot out of holsters and aimed at Thomas. His form loomed larger and his features came into stark relief. The dark hollows of his eyes turned in the direction of the cops.

"I'd put those guns away, if I were you," I told them. "If I had to guess, I'd say he doesn't like weapons."

Ben's Glock disappeared quickly into his holster. Tristan assumed the stance, legs spread apart, both hands clutching and aiming his gun.

"What's wrong with you?" he snarled at his partner. "Can't you see it's a trick? These jokesters think they're funny. One of them is over there pretending to be a ghost."

If only.

The Wiccans clustered together. Once over their initial shock, they were thrilled. A real spirit had come through from the other side.

Thomas had been laid in the ground in his best outfit. His ruffled shirt gleamed white under a dark tailcoat that looked like wool. Since he hovered over his table tombstone, his tall boots were visible over narrow trousers. If he'd worn a hat to the grave, he left it there, and his white hair was tied back from his face. Funny his clothes hadn't deteriorated in the past 150 years.

Yikes, what was I thinking? Why should his clothing be hanging in rags when his face and body looked no worse than the day he was buried? I assumed, since I wasn't there. This was

Thomas's spirit, not a freaking zombie.

"Please put that gun away, Officer," Garnet implored. "He comes in peace. If you frighten him with a weapon that didn't exist during his lifetime, he may disappear. We may never have this opportunity again."

Tristan didn't so much as flinch at the thought of a spirit. His gun continued to point unwaveringly at Thomas. "Are you for real, ma'am? There are no such things as ghosts. If you people didn't orchestrate this, someone else is playing tricks on you."

Garnet was a responsible business owner, unused to being questioned. "Young man, I will have your photo and badge number, and take this up with Chief Redfern at the next Police Board meeting, of which I am a member." Her flash went off in Tristan's face.

"Could be teenagers," I agreed, although I thought no such thing, just hoping to diffuse the situation. "In which case, you are pointing your weapon at a perfectly harmless kid. You know you have to fill in a report for simply pulling your gun out of its holster, right? If you discharge it, even accidentally, well, all hell will rain down on you, starting with Chief Neil Redfern." Since Ben pulled his gun and as quickly put it away, I planned to ignore his part in this fiasco if called upon as a witness.

The coyotes picked that moment to growl. Out came Ben's gun again. He was on his own now.

Tristan's gun swung in an arc across the mob of Wiccans and one innocent observer — me — until it aimed at the coyotes. I noticed his trigger finger tighten and called out, "No! You can't shoot coyotes in Southern Ontario unless they are a direct danger to yourself or others, or you're a farmer protecting livestock. There's a flipping fence between the animals and us. You will be bound over for prosecution if you kill or injure one." I may have flowered up the wording but, essentially, what I said was true.

Tristan's eyes had a decidedly wild look in them. I wasn't sure he heard me. In front of him were two wild animals, basically taunting him. The thing behind him wasn't a teenager masquerading as a spirit from the 1880s, and he knew it.

I had a bad feeling this idiot might shoot something in the next minute or two. More likely a someone.

CHAPTER 10

TO LIGHTEN THE MOOD and possibly save a life, I nudged Ciera. "So, is the Veil over there beside Thomas Warrick's grave? Should we expect more spirits of the cemetery residents to join us? How many spirits usually come to a Samhain celebration? I don't think we have many cakes left."

Ciera's mouth opened and closed, but no words came out. I herded the Wiccans behind the two cops as far back as possible without pressing them against the fence. The wavering Glocks made me nervous. I'd rather face Thomas than two rookies, armed and scared shitless.

I didn't want to send these gun-wielding minions of the law into overdrive by pointing out that at least three tombstones close to Thomas glowed softly. Any second, Ciera and Chesley would have their spirit gathering.

"Thomas is staring at your bicorn, Chesley." Don't ask me how I knew that. "If I were you, I'd remove it. There may have been hard feelings between the settlers and the British military in this County after the War of 1812."

Chesley whipped off his hat and tossed it at the fence. One of the coyotes drew back and snarled. This brought the guns back to the fence line. If there had been any cell reception in this forgotten corner of the township, I'd have called Neil. As

49

it was, the Wiccans and my blameless self were at the mercy of two fledgling cops and a rising mutiny of spirits set to come forth from the far side of the Veil, whatever and wherever the hell that was. I believed it to be a bad idea, spirits and the living intermingling.

I had an idea. "The coyotes must be hungry. How about we feed them some seed cakes? Then, maybe they'll go away. There can't be anything in the cakes that will harm wildlife."

Ian Mueller, the owner of the Kinky Tattoo Parlour said, "Coyotes eat other animals including cats and small dogs if they can grab one." Pause for collective gasp of horror. "If you feed them, they'll get used to getting food from humans and even follow you home."

Better than bullets flying around willy-nilly. I gathered up a handful of cakes and walked slowly to the coyotes. The wire fence was five feet high or so, including the rolls of rusted barbed wire strung along the top. I tossed the cakes, one at a time, over the barbed wire, leaving a half dozen for Thomas and the other spirits who would show up if we didn't get the hell out of there, like now.

The coyotes ate the cakes and licked their chops. Strange, I hadn't found them that good. "Shoo, now, no more for you. Go home."

They licked their snouts again and stood firm. The back of my neck felt prickly and I turned around, expecting a couple more spirits to be standing beside Thomas. Not yet, although the same graves glowed, and Thomas hovered above his, seemingly interested in the goings-on. Tristan's gun caused me more discomfort.

I think he decided to ignore the Veil and Thomas, focusing

on a threat he understood. Or, misunderstood in this instance. The coyotes were minding their own business, waiting expectantly for more treats, ignoring the weapon trained on them.

Big mistake on my part to feed them. "Hey," I said to the Wiccans. "We should pack up now and leave. Immediately. Let's move it."

Didn't happen.

"Bliss, we may never get another opportunity to see a spirit of the dead come through the Veil during a Samhain celebration. Do you know how rare this is?" Ciera's expression became more determined. Chesley pressed her shoulder, looking scared but supportive.

"What if the entire cemetery rises," I yelled at her. "They outnumber us twenty to one."

"They can't hurt us, Bliss." Garnet Maybe stood beside Ciera. "This will be a communion of souls, both past and present."

"You think they can talk to you?" Ben asked.

"Of course not," Garnet snapped at him, ignoring the guns wavering in both cops' hands. "We will simply exist together for a time before the spirits return to their side of the Veil."

She gave Tristan a hard look. "Now, if you officers will take your weapons and leave, it may not be too late for our gathering. You are creating a hostile environment for the spirits."

"Please take Bliss with you," Chesley added. "She doesn't exude the proper attitude for a peaceful assembly of living and non-living essences."

"Yeah, we probably should." Tristan holstered his gun, then

pulled it out again a second later. "Chief Redfern might go easier on us if we rescue his wife from these ... these ..."

"Flakes?" Ben said in a whisper. Amazing how sound carries at night in the countryside. "Good idea."

Tristan grabbed my arm.

"Here now," I said, kicking him in the shin, hard enough so he let me go. "I'm not going anywhere with you. I'm responsible for what happens in this cemetery." Now that I had a possible ride out of the ninth circle of Hell, I wasn't anxious to leave. My terms or no go.

"You assaulted a police officer." Tristan's eyes widened at my blatant violation of the Criminal Code.

"Freaking good luck with that one," I told him. "Don't touch me again."

Ciera laid her hand gently on my arm. "Ches is right, Bliss. You can come back for your car tomorrow. I'm afraid your disbelief may interfere with the spirit manifestation."

"What are you talking about? We already have one spirit. I can't believe you want more." I turned to point at Thomas. "Oh, crap."

Heads turned; everyone gasped; a few shrieked.

Hands neatly folded across her bosom, a spirit lady hovered on the very tip of the tall Celtic cross next to Thomas's grave.

CHAPTER 11

THOMAS AND HIS NEIGHBOUR didn't acknowledge one another, both bobbing gently through the haze that now encompassed the cemetery. I couldn't remember her name but she hadn't been Thomas's wife. He was alone in his grave. I think that's one of the reasons I spent so many Friday nights sprawled across Thomas's tomb — he was sure to be glad of the company. Plus, his flat surface was perfect for star-gazing and, okay, slamming tequila.

This time I was ready and didn't freeze to the ground. I edged my phone from my tote and took a few pics. The age-old question of whether spirits can be photographed would finally be answered.

Whoops. The top halves of Thomas and the lady swiveled in my direction. Their feet remained tethered to their graves. I put my phone away and pulled the hood over my head.

Just because they were currently fastened to their tombs, didn't mean they couldn't gather enough energy to move closer. Most of the Wiccans had their phones out and were taking shots of the ghosts who, thankfully, seemed to forget about one little Reaper and faced the white-clad throng.

"Put your phones away, guys," I said. "They don't like the flashes of light."

Phones disappeared. The cops? They turned their backs on the coyotes that, I noted with detached interest, had now swelled to a pack of six. The coyotes seemed fascinated by the spirits and sat quietly in a row, like they were watching a stage show.

Tristan and Ben aimed their weapons at the spirits. Kind of funny, really. They must know by now that even the most skilled human magician couldn't contrive these effects. I expected to have a major meltdown later, but right now, it was weird how I accepted the reality of spirits. I was even okay with a pack of predators at my back.

"Maybe you should go over there and check to see if it's a bunch of teenagers playing tricks on us," I suggested. I'd risk the ire of Thomas and the lady to get a shot of that.

Tristan looked at me and I raised my eyebrows in a challenge. "I understand if you're too scared." Anything to get these guns away from real people.

"Come on, Ben," he ordered.

Since they were both rookie constables, Ben could have told his friend to shove it, but he dutifully followed. Guns shook in their hands.

They took three steps before a commanding voice called from the direction of Darkwood's entrance, "Secure your weapons at once and stand down."

CHAPTER 12

FINALLY, A SANE COP. For a big guy, Neil moves quietly. He's always sneaking up behind me, catching me wallowing in a bubble bath while shaving my legs and belting out the words to Eminem's *The Way I Am*. Scares the shit out of me. He apologizes, but still asks me to keep it down. He's trying to sleep, or think, or eat, or watch a hockey game, or all four at the same time.

Still, how did he manage to enter Darkwood without snapping a twig when no one was speaking or squealing? Maybe the hammering of our hearts concealed his passage.

He spotted the spirits immediately, and I watched for his reaction. His expression reminded me of someone who just ate a glass and lettuce sandwich. I scanned the cemetery for newcomers but, so far, Thomas and the lady were the only two who had parted the Veil.

Neil is the most rational man to walk the earth and I was interested to see how he'd handle a key shift in his reality such as spirits floating over their long-buried bones. So far, he pretended not to notice and decided to rake over his rookies. Very carefully, since members of the public were present.

"Officers McNally and Minor. Why did you two have your guns out? Do you know the paperwork that is involved when an officer draws his weapon?"

"We perceived a threat, sir." Tristan drew to attention and all but saluted.

"To our persons and the public," added Ben who obviously paid attention in class at the Police Academy, but in all likelihood barely scraped through the practical training.

Neil glanced over at the coyote pack which now numbered eight members. Flickers of firelight danced in their white eyeshine, and they ignored the living, straining against the fence to focus on the dead.

Tristan pointed at me. "She said we couldn't shoot coyotes."

I pointed my finger right back. "Truth. Deal with it."

Neil still wore the black jeans and tee shirt, with a black, padded jacket. If it wasn't for his blond hair, he wouldn't show up in the dark. The spirits were more visible than him. Tucked up against his ass, his home gun was safely holstered, and he left it where it was. Setting an example.

"Why are you out here in the first place? And, why are you together instead of patrolling with your training officers?"

He kept his voice low, and I edged closer to catch the words he didn't want me or the Wiccans to hear.

Ben's mouth opened and closed but, before he formed words, Tristan boldly walked into the lion's den.

"Sergeants Vanderbloom and Rundell were called to assist the OPP in a multi-car pileup on the highway outside town. Sergeant Rundell said he didn't want us cluttering the scene."

"And, what orders did they leave you?"

Before either of the hapless, newly-badged cops had a chance to reply, Neil held up a hand. He turned to the Wiccans who were torn between keeping watchful eyes on the growing pack of coyotes, basking in the essence of two spirits from beyond the Veil, and trying to hear the obnoxious cops told off by their boss.

Neil addressed Ciera, "Miss Dorlan, I assume you've completed your ceremony. Would you start packing up and prepare for departure? I trust you brought plenty of water to douse the fire. Don't worry about the coyotes; they'll disperse as soon as we're gone."

Like city cop knew anything about wildlife in the depths of Bruce County. He avoided any mention of the spirits that showed no sign of fading back to where they came from. If anything, Thomas and the lady had moved ever-so-slightly closer to us.

By the time he faced his two troublemakers again, I'd inched close enough to hear more clearly. He noticed me but chose not to acknowledge my presence.

"Speak," he told them. Then, "Wait, I should make a note of this or I'm sure to forget at least a couple of points by tomorrow morning." He ever-so-slowly took out his phone and tapped at it. "I want to see you both promptly at ten a.m. I expect two hours may be enough time for me to write up a preliminary report."

By this time, Ben and Tristan were sweating mightily in the autumn chill, rendered colder by the spirits who, what the hell, yes they were, moving even closer to the dampened remnants of the fire.

"Well?" Neil enquired. At six-two, he was barely an inch or so taller than both Ben and Tristan but he appeared to tower over them.

"Uh," Ben responded, "I forget the question."

"What were your orders when your training officers left to attend a serious accident scene?"

Tristan knew the answer to that one. "Patrol the main street and radio them if we see any vandalism or other violation."

"But, do not intervene," Ben added.

"Instead, without permission, you took a scout, followed a group of citizens out of town, and interfered in their religious freedom. Then, you drew your weapons without a perceived threat to the public or yourselves. Does that about cover it?"

"Yes," Tristan answered quickly.

Ben took a few extra seconds. "That's all I can think of."

"Glad I'm not either of you," Neil said. "It's bad enough I'm responsible for your conduct, which isn't going down well with me. At the very least, this stunt will extend your probationary period."

He stared at his naughty boys until they fidgeted and sweated more freely. Finally, he said, "Drive the scout back to the station and go home."

I snickered as Ben held up his hand. "Uh, thank you, sir. But, we don't know how to get back to the station from here. The GPS is fuc... screwed up, due to go in for repairs tomorrow. Which is why we borrowed it. We followed the last vehicle in the procession."

"Without lights or sirens," Tristan contributed, as though that made it all okay. I laughed out loud.

"How did you find us?" Ben asked. "There's no cell coverage out here. Wherever this is."

Neil didn't respond, but I knew how he found us — or

me, to be more accurate. After a loud negotiation a few months ago, I'd allowed him to buy a plug-in tracker, instead of a permanent, wired-in stalker, for my vehicle. Now, when I ventured into areas with no GPS or cell phone coverage to perform my cemetery inspections, I plugged it in.

This made my solitary trips into the far reaches of the township far less pleasurable. If my vehicle was stationary too long, I knew he'd send out a scout or three to find out why. Or worse, find me himself. Nowadays, I didn't have time to saunter at leisure among the graves searching out invasive ivy or deliberate vandalism, or anything in between, enjoying the peace of the burial grounds. And, talking to the residents. I must have plugged in the tracker automatically when I left the greenhouse.

CHAPTER 13

GARNET TRAILED BEHIND Neil, yammering at him about calling a special meeting of the Police Board to discuss his two unsuitable hires. He nodded and bent to fold the repast table to help move the Wiccans along. A few doused the fire with water from a cooler and stirred the embers, but most stood, transfixed, as Thomas drew nearer and larger. I snatched up my scraped-clean dip bowl, prepared to run.

The Wiccans' phones took shots that wouldn't show anything except irregular ovals of white light, if my photos were anything to go by. Nothing even a want-to-believe sceptic couldn't refute.

Thomas hovered six inches off the ground less than 30 metres away. The lady, probably knowing her place as a woman in her timeline, weaved back and forth but stayed put atop her Celtic cross. Here I'd been thinking this shitshow from beyond the grave was winding down.

A quick glance around the burial place confirmed no other spirits had yet journeyed through the Veil, although at least half of the hundred plus graves radiated that odd light. Strange that the luminosity didn't disperse the fog and shadows filling the spaces between the tombstones. I couldn't make out the rusted wrought iron fence that surrounded three sides of the cemetery. Even the barbed wire fence and the looming corn stalks a few metres away disappeared within the encompassing mist. As had the coyotes' forms. But, their eyes fixed on Thomas and shone dully. I counted them. Fifteen.

What? Not sixteen? I counted again. Still fifteen. Unless one of the coyotes lost an eye, something else had joined them. I'd go with a one-eyed coyote.

Neil steadfastly refused to look at, or acknowledge, the presence of two spirits in Darkwood. There was a growing possibility that the entire resident population would shortly cross the Veil and join the cemetery hoedown. I'd like to see him ignore a hundred spectres, except I didn't want to be around when it happened.

"Are you still here? Go," he commanded Ben and Tristan. "Sit in the scout and wait for everyone else to pull out. You follow at the end." He watched while the well-chastised cops trudged towards the cemetery pillars.

"Wait," Ciera called. She rushed along the path to intercept the cops. "You can't just walk out of a cemetery where spirits have manifested."

The boys halted so abruptly at the entrance — or exit, same diff — Ben ran into the back of Tristan.

"What do you mean? Why can't we?" Ben asked, his voice squeaky, reminding me both cops were still in their early twenties, without fully-matured pre-frontal lobes. Their training officers should have locked them in a cell before leaving for the emergency call-out.

I was impressed with Ciera. She stood, like a Viking queen at the bow of a warship, her formidable chest heaving with power.

She reached out and pulled Ben and Tristan away from the pillars. "You must perform the ritual and speak the correct words before you leave."

"So, what'll happen if I don't?" Such a rebel. Tristan pulled his arm free and prepared to stride from the cemetery while he had his dignity. In his mind, he still had a modicum left. I moved away from the security of the obelisk tomb and kicked through the dried grass towards the trio. I needed to hear this in case I had to depart without warning.

"Go ahead, then," Ciera challenged him. "The spirits are here at our invitation. Do you want one to follow you home? If that happens, it's a bitch to get rid of. If ever."

CHAPTER 14

TRISTAN THREW A GLANCE in Neil's direction and lowered his voice, although the swirling fog caused his words to echo from the tombstones and reach the ears of the rest of the Wiccans. Neil continued to help them pack up, his back to Thomas, shrugging his shoulders like he felt the air becoming icier the closer Thomas drifted.

"Okay, what do we have to say?" Tristan hugged a sagging stone pillar and lifted one leg. Bet this kid would never again set foot in a cemetery after dark. He looked past Ciera and froze.

Thomas loomed larger and closer to Neil and the Wiccans. I pressed against the second pillar, longing to run to safety right then. Except I didn't know the words yet. And, I couldn't leave my husband to the consequences of his stubborn, linear brain.

Ciera held the back of Ben's jacket with one hand. With the other, she jerked Tristan safely back inside the cemetery. "Stand still, both of you. This will only take a second."

A coyote barked, drowning out Ciera's words. Another yelped, followed by a symphony of yips and whines. Don't let anyone tell you that only wolves howl. Uh-Uh, nope. Soon, the entire pack followed the howler, singly and in unison. The fog amplified the eerie sound until the howls filled Darkwood.

Coyotes communicate with each other using various calls, and I had a feeling they were warning the rest of their pack to stay clear of the cemetery tonight.

On the other hand, maybe they were warning us. No need. We got the message. A stampede of human feet beat their way towards the exit. Chesley led the charge, the rest of the Wiccans in the middle, and Neil at the end carrying a folded table he handed off to Ian Mueller. Thomas followed slowly, his torso leaning forward, as though trying to move faster, faster. Tendrils of vapour wove around his form, concealing his facial features. What the hell did his spirit want with us? Unless Thomas had been a sorcerer in life, he couldn't possess anyone. The lady in her long dress trailed slowly behind.

I itched to crawl over Ciera and the rookies to be first out of this haunted place and leave the unnatural phantoms behind. If only I could see Thomas's expression. Was it malevolent? Curious? Lonely? Did he even have a face?

My knees wobbled when a hand landed on my shoulder. I may have screeched a little before the hand covered my mouth and a voice whispered in my ear. "Quiet. We don't want to cause panic in here. Stick with me."

He didn't have to tell me twice. I huddled up to Neil's body and peeked around to see Thomas's whereabout. Creeping up. Past time to go.

I reached out and prodded Ciera. "Let's get this done. The spirits, for anyone who cares to observe ...," I glanced up at Neil's chin, "... are closing in. Tell us what to say, fast."

She clutched the two young cops in an iron grip. She let go of Ben, and placed her hands on Tristan's shoulders to move him around so his back faced the exit.

"Everybody! Each of you must say these words as you back out of the cemetery. Ready?"

At this point, my eyes were rolling around in my head with frustration. "We're running out of time. Let's move it."

"Repeat these words," Ciera directed Tristan. "Meaningfully. 'No spirit shall follow me from this place.' Got it?"

"No spirit shall follow me from this place," Tristan mumbled as he backed from under the arch of stone over the ancient pillars.

Ben closely followed him after repeating the words. Their boots crackled in the dead grass as they headed for their scout at a clip worthy of their Police Academy boot camp.

One by one, each with their load of ceremonial supplies and leftover mead, the Wiccans turned their backs to the exit and stepped out of the cemetery. "No spirit shall follow me from this place." They'd left the pumpkins and gourds behind. Crap. Now I'd have to come back and clean up. Four dirt-encrusted tequila bottles clanged together in my tote.

I memorized the words, not for just my turn tonight, but for all future forays into the hidden and abandoned burial grounds of the township. I was lucky my house wasn't filled with displaced spirits following me back from my official inspections.

Neil shouted after the departing witches, "Back out carefully and line up your vehicles, in the middle of the road if necessary. Bliss will lead us back to town. I'll follow her, with the rest of you next, and the scout will be at the rear. If you head off on your own, I don't care, but don't expect a search party to come looking for you."

"That's telling them," I murmured. We were alone in Darkwood with Ciera.

CHAPTER 15

THE COYOTES FELL QUIET. Not one at a time, but together and abruptly. I preferred the howling.

From this distance, I couldn't see the *fifteen* eyes, but heard the pack's departure loud and clear. For the record, coyotes aren't as quiet as you may think. Oh, they try, but a dry twig is always ready to be trod on, even by sure-footed forest predators.

With a fearful look at Thomas and the lady, enveloped in mist and floating nearer, Ciera motioned us to leave. A Wiccan High Priestess leaves no one behind. Neither does a career cop who would walk through a clearly visible spirit manifestation and not admit there was any such thing in existence. Impasse.

I turned Ciera around and stationed her under Darkwood's arch. "Leave. We'll be right behind you."

She looked directly at Redfern as she recited the protective words, "No spirit shall follow me from this place. Blessed Be."

Clear of the cemetery, she whipped around and marched to her vehicle without looking back. Yeah, she had his number.

I grasped Neil's arm. "We'll do this together."

Neil tried to go around me, reaching for my hand at the same time. "Come on. This is nonsense.

I pushed on him. Surprised, he fell back.

Pointing over his shoulder, I said. "Turn around and look. If you think Thomas or his lovely friend are coming home with us, think again."

He did turn around. He did take a good look. Thomas wavered not 15 metres away, growing more distinct every moment. Now, I recognized the expression on Thomas's face — hunger, longing, with a smidge of malevolence. If I had to guess, he hadn't been an affable man in life. More likely a hanging judge.

"You either say the words and back out, or I'm staying right here until daybreak. By then, I could be possessed or dragged back to the other side of the Veil with Thomas and the other one, but they will not follow us home." The unearthly chill emanating from the spirits cut through my reaper robe and curled around my bones.

Neil couldn't seem to rip his gaze away from the *non-spirits*. "I will pick you up and carry you out."

"I don't recommend it unless you want an unwelcome passenger in your back seat on the drive home. He doesn't seem to like you." Indeed, Thomas turned in Neil's direction and reached out, not quite able to reach him, yet.

That did it. He caved.

"Okay, I'll humour you. I'll do it, but you go first."

"Nope. You first. I'll be right behind you." Neil was obstinate and a lot of work, but I loved him. And, I didn't want Thomas as a housemate the rest of my life.

Someone in the line of vehicles outside the gates honked their horn. Thomas didn't react but I called over my shoulder, "Shut up!" Let's not antagonize the ghosts. Have I mentioned, this is the last time I accompanied the Wiccans to one of their festivals or solstices? Also, they weren't using my cemeteries to celebrate in, ever. Enticing the dead from their eternal rest was a definite no-no from this night forward.

Neil gave in, and mumbled, "No spirit shall follow me from this place." He backed out and yelled at me to hurry up.

I tuned him out and addressed the spirits. "You go back, now, Thomas and whoever you are, lady. I'm sure the place you've spent the last 150 years is much nicer than today's world." Unless it was Hell. Best to be positive in case they forgot where they came from. "Return and tell your friends and family how awful it is here. No reason for anyone to haunt the living. We have enough problems ..."

"Bliss!"

"Fine!" I placed one foot behind the other until I stood directly under Darkwood's arch. "No spirit shall follow me from this place." Just for good measure, I threw in a 'Blessed Be,' like a real witch.

I got one foot on the other side before Neil grabbed me and hustled me towards my Matrix. He opened the driver's door and boosted me in. "I'll line everyone else up and leave a gap for you to take the spot in front of me. Don't back up until I give you the go-ahead."

In my rear mirror I watched him reach into his red Jeep, place his portable whirly-light on the roof and walk along the line of vehicles, leaning into each driver's window. Slowly, the vehicles backed up until space for his Jeep and my Matrix cleared. I made the mistake of looking back at Darkwood. Reaction was setting in, and my entire body shuddered.

Although the lady was pulling back and fading, Thomas made it as far as the arch, his arms reaching through. Thank

Heaven, or the Underworld, whichever was most present tonight, his body was unable to follow. I rolled my window down and stood on my seat to lean out. "Go back, Thomas. You can't follow. Sorry the Wiccan celebration brought you through the Veil. Big mistake. Please don't haunt anyone who comes to visit the cemetery ..."

Neil laid on his horn from outside his Jeep, then hollered, "Come on, Bliss. Let's go." He started up his whirly and gave me another blast.

What a pain in the ass. Henceforth, he'd totally deny there was a spirit in the cemetery and insist we all suffered from toxic mold sweeping in from the cornfield or another improbable cause for hallucinations. As I backed carefully out of the overgrown lane that had once served as the ceremonial approach to Darkwood, I stopped once more to take a look at the gates. Thomas had disappeared.

I checked my back seat in case he teleported. Finding it unoccupied, I turned my headlights off and peered into the cemetery. Inside the confines of the rusted wrought iron railings, a faint glow moved slowly away from the entrance towards the area of the cemetery where Thomas's grave lay waiting for him.

Just ask me if I'd ever set foot in Darkwood again. Bears or porcupines would eat the pumpkins and gourds and be happy for the change in diet. Fifty-fifty chance Darkwood wasn't within Lockport's jurisdiction anyway. The only reason I included it on my inspection rounds was to reminisce for a few minutes about my teen years. Highly over-rated, nostalgia.

CHAPTER 16

NEIL LINED US UP ON the road with me in front as per his perception I was the only one who knew where we were. He wasn't wrong; without the tracker, he would never have found me.

For the second time, he moved from car to car, having a word with each driver, probably reinforcing his edict to stay in place or risk being lost forever in the forest. Darkwood Burial Ground was well named. On the other hand, he may have warned them not to speak of what happened this Halloween night to anyone outside their circle and to stay out of cemeteries. If I knew my Wiccans, they'd try to conjure up a spirit or two every Samhain from now on. It would be up to me to deflect them lest they sneak off to another cemetery and perform the same ritual. How I'd accomplish that without tagging along was a problem for next year.

When Neil rapped on my window, I jumped a foot. I lowered the window and glanced back at Darkwood. Nary a glimmer nor a glow shone from the shadows within. With any luck, Thomas had returned to his grave as instructed.

"Can I have the whirly on my roof?" I asked. "I'm in front. It's only reasonable that I ..."

"Certainly not. I've instructed the other drivers to

maintain a car's length between them. You drive a steady 30 kph. Once we're back in Lockport, the others will use their indicators when they wish to leave the line."

"Yessir. Anything else? It's not like we're a million miles from civilization."

"I know you used a circuitous route to bring these people here, and I'd prefer you to take us back the same way. The last thing I want is for them to find this place again. It's bad enough you know where it is."

"Okay, well, if that's all ..."

"Make sure your Bluetooth is turned on."

I paused my window half-way up. "There's no cell reception for miles."

"I know that but, when there is, I might want to talk to you."

No doubt about that. He got into his Jeep and gave me a horn blast. Off we went, *snailing* along at 30 kph.

With a few miles between me and Darkwood Burial Ground, I relaxed and stopped glancing at my back seat. I did my best to forget Neil, too. At times, he chewed off my last nerve; and that's the truth.

On the left, white glowing eyes peered from the thick forest. Neil had neglected to mention a plan if deer ran across my path. If I stopped to let them cross, he was skilled enough not to rear-end me but, somewhere down the line, a series of front and rear bumpers would collide. The idiot rookies would make sure of that.

Moot point. Deer eyeshine was yellow. We lived down a country road on the south side of Lockport and I was used to braking for deer after dusk. These white eyes didn't belong to deer.

A coyote broke from the tree line and lifted his head to watch us pass. Just in time, I stopped my foot from slamming on the brake. Neil's calm voice filled the front seat. "Those are coyotes. Keep driving. They won't jump into the road."

Super. Cell reception. My voice came out a mousy squeak. "They're the same coyotes from the cemetery."

"I doubt it."

The pack stayed ahead of us and, since we travelled at the speed of drying polar bear snot, I managed to count the eyes. Fifteen.

It *was* the same coyote pack. I wanted to be in my own bed, with my irascible yet muscular, hot husband to comfort me. Although I'd rip out my own nails before I admitted to such a girly wish.

Neil was city-born and bred, moving to Lockport less than five years ago to take up the job of police chief — the youngest chief in Lockport history, but that's another story. In any case, I had to keep in mind he knew nothing about wildlife. The coyote pack left the forest and ran alongside my vehicle.

They didn't need to break into a gallop to keep up, just maintained an easy lope. The big guy in front turned his head to look at me. One eye. I rolled my window down and took a good look. Scar tissue covered the space where the other eye should be. A seasoned warrior, alpha male. The female following close behind would be his mate, and the rest their grown offspring.

And, who the hell cared about the family dynamics of a coyote pack? They slunk silently alongside our motorcade, the leader keeping pace with me.

A thought hit my brain so hard, I felt my forehead bend. Why hadn't I realized this before? The pack hadn't been threatening us in the cemetery. They had been protecting us from a supernatural force the best they knew how. They followed us to ensure we got safely away from Darkwood. That sounded ridiculous when I ran it through my mind, but I believed it.

Sure enough, as soon as we turned left at the highway that would take us to the southern edge of Lockport, the pack halted at the stop sign. They gathered together and gave one long, loud howl, warning us to stay away from Darkwood when the Veil was thin. I lost sight of them after that but said to Neil, "Give those doggies a goodbye blast on your siren to thank them for the escort. Not too loud."

"I have no siren in my personal vehicle," came the repressive reply. But, he pressed his horn lightly, bless his heart.

We drove a few more miles and, as we approached Concession Rd 12 that led to our home, I asked, "Do you want me to turn?" As in, do we want all these witches and rookies in our back yard?

CHAPTER 17

"KEEP GOING."

We passed the Lockport welcome sign. I chortled when I noticed someone had crossed out "Population: 7,000" and spray painted a prone stick figure with crosses for eyes. Classic.

"I suppose you did the same thing every Halloween when you were a wild child?" Neil's voice sounded more exhausted than annoyed. I felt a little sorry for him until I remembered I had to be at the greenhouse for nine o'clock that morning to browbeat deadbeat customers, only one hour after he was due at the station to boss everyone around from the comfort of his padded, leather office chair.

"I must confess I did, a few times, ages fourteen through seventeen. After that, we passed the torch to the younger kids."

"Tomorrow, Municipal Works will waste resources removing the paint when they have better things to do."

"They're used to it. Probably did it themselves when they were teenagers. It's a Lockport Halloween tradition. When can we turn around?"

"When we escort the last vehicle to their driveway. Keep driving."

Chesley and Ciera turned left on Harbour Street. I guessed they would spend the rest of the night in her tiny apartment above her Above and Below Shop, discussing the success of dragging a couple of reluctant souls across the Veil. One by one, the remaining half dozen cars left the parade until only me, Neil, and the rookie duo remained.

I didn't get to turn around until a mile before the welcome sign on the north end of Lockport. We'd arrived at the new municipal complex, a spacious building that housed not only the police station, but the town offices and mayoral headquarters.

I figured Neil would want to stop and chew out Tristan and Ben. I didn't want to miss it, so I stopped and waited while the scout turned into the police parking lot behind the building.

Neil didn't follow. "Let's get home," he instructed.

Back through the deserted centre core we travelled. Even the die-hard troublemakers had given up and gone home to bed. A few homeowners had forgotten to bring in their jack-o'-lanterns, and they sat, forlorn and sad, on front porches and sidewalks.

"I'm going to pick up the pace a little," I informed Neil. "I could walk home faster than this."

"As long as you don't go over the speed limit," he replied.

I was already ten kph over, but whatever. We proceeded sedately until we reached the gates of our driveway. I gunned my motor, then slammed on the brakes in time to avoid the waters of the bay lapping at the front lawn. I did that all the time, just for fun, but never when Neil was around. Couldn't resist tonight.

Should have known I wouldn't get a reaction.

"You might want to back up a few yards. Your front tires are underwater," he called from the front door, entering the code on the keypad to let himself in, then the keypad to disable the security alarm. Different numbers, of course, which he changed monthly.

By the time, I backed up the Matrix and got out, the house was ablaze with light. So was the forest.

I looked again. The forest surrounding our outbuildings wasn't lit up like a night baseball game exactly but, hell, there were eyes staring back at me. White eyes. I didn't stay to count them.

I ran through the door, straight into Neil who performed his nightly ritual of re-setting the alarm. "The coyotes are here. In the woods. How do they know where we live? Do you think they'll take up residence?"

"Probably wolves. We've had reports of packs spotted closer to town than out here."

"I know the difference between coyote and wolf eyes. I want to move back to town," I muttered. That was a losing battle. Neil loved country living — lake, forest, critters. Surprising for a city boy.

"No, you don't. Remember all the nosy neighbours?" He put his arm around me and led me to the bedroom.

We settled into bed and turned off the lights. Neil took his usual three seconds to fall asleep.

I prodded him awake again. "We need to talk about what we saw in the cemetery tonight."

"I don't think so. Those so-called ghosts are nothing but blank projections. I'm not saying your Wiccan friends didn't conjure up a weird energy field with the bongos and mead, but no souls crossed the Great Divide. Not possible. I don't want to talk about it ever again. Got it?"

Soft, deep breathing followed. He never snored, which was about all he had going for him right now. Ghost denier.

I lay rigidly awake, jittery from the spirit shenanigans at the cemetery, remembering what Ciera said about Samhain.

Samhain is observed from sunset on October 31st to sunset on November 1st. It was officially November 1st. Therefore, Thomas wasn't required to return to his grave tonight, or this morning to be more accurate, when we left Darkwood. The Veil wouldn't close until tomorrow — dammit, I meant this evening — at sunset. Those sneaky Wiccans might ...

I poked Neil.

"What! You're going to drive me to an early grave."

"You have to place the Wiccans in protective custody until tomorrow at sunset. So they can't go back to Darkwood."

He rolled onto his back. "Really? And, why is that?"

I told him. He wasn't buying it.

"Good night, my love," he said, and fell asleep again.

Screw this. I got up and made myself a cup of pumpkin spice tea. I sat in bed with my back against the headboard and tried to quiet my brain. I sipped the tea and, slowly, I calmed.

Neil rolled over and, in the darkness, the whites of his eyes blinked at me. "I knew I smelled something obnoxious. Your blood type must be pumpkin spice by now."

"Get used to it ..."

"Any taco dip left?"

"Are you kidding? Someone licked the bowl clean."

From the woods outside, an owl hooted. "There you are," he said sleepily, patting my leg. "It's official. Halloween is over."

The hoot had scarcely faded away when the mournful howl

of a lone coyote followed. Seconds later, an entire pack took up the call. They'd stay until sunset tomorrow — dammit, today. Would they follow me to work? How would I explain that to everyone? It wasn't even my fault.

Neil's eyes snapped open again.

I scooted over until my body pressed against his. "Halloween may be officially finished for another year," I told him. "But the Veil hasn't closed on Samhain."

The End

Happy Halloween.

See you on the other side of Samhain!

APPRECIATION

HEARTFELT THANKS TO my lifelong friend and supreme beta reader, Maureen. She's always up for reading my books multiple times to catch plot holes and awkward phrases, or those elements that just don't fit. Despite my imperfections as a writer, she seems to enjoy what she reads!

My gratitude is boundless, Maureen.

NOTE FROM THE AUTHOR

REAPER BLISS IS A BLISS and Neil Halloween/Samhain special.

For more of Bliss Moonbeam Cornwall and Police Chief Neil Redfern, check out the Cornwall & Redfern Mystery series, featuring small-town mystery, humour, murder, and more than a touch of romance.

Bliss takes sass to a whole new level as she kicks butt and takes no prisoners. Neil? He tries to contain the damage while solving murders and other crimes. Together, they're irresistible (if I do say so myself).

If you enjoyed REAPER BLISS or any of the other books in the series, please consider leaving a review. That will make me dance for joy. Really, you should see me!

www.gloriaferris.com

gloriaferriswrites@gmail.com

A final note: For your reading pleasure, I have included the first chapter of SKULL GARDEN, Book 3 of the Cornwall & Redfern Mysteries.

Hope you like it.

ALSO BY GLORIA FERRIS

The Cornwall & Redfern Mysteries
CORPSE FLOWER
SHROUD OF ROSES
SKULL GARDEN
WEDDED BLISS (Novelette)
DARK BLOSSOMING
REAPER BLISS (Halloween Novelette)
The Blood Series (YA Contemporary Fantasy)
BLOOD PATCH
BLOOD SHIELD
The Blair & Piermont Crime Thriller Series
(with Donna Warner)
TARGETED
DEATH'S FOOTPRINT
The Mechanic Falls Gem Caper Series
By Ferris Tremain
(Gloria Ferris & Jamie Tremain)
WORLDS MAY CHANGE
TEQUILA CLAUS (A Christmas Special Novella)

ABOUT THE AUTHOR

GLORIA BEGAN HER WRITING career as a procedure writer at a nuclear power plant. Sure, it was an exciting job, but there's just so much you can do with prompts like, "Do NOT Press PB47," or "ACTIVATE the Evacuation Alarm and RUN!"

So, Gloria turned to fiction writing and is now the award-winning author of the humorous Cornwall & Redfern Mysteries; a co-written suspense series; and a YA contemporary fantasy series. She also co-writes the Mechanic Falls Gem Capers with author Jamie Tremain. Every so often, she'll write a short story just for the heck of it.

She has fully embraced her dark side but doesn't take it too seriously. She loves abandoned cemeteries, and all things "skull", managing to work one or both of these elements into her books. She once made an honest attempt to write a serious book, but that didn't go well, so now she lets her snarky and, occasionally, inappropriate humour prevail.

Gloria lives in southwestern Ontario.

SKULL GARDEN
(Chapter 1)

By Gloria Ferris

I EASED THE SAVAGE to the edge of the pavement and cut the engine. Chesley swung a lanky leg over my head and hopped off the back seat. While he checked his teeth for bugs, I spread a hand-drawn map across the seat. "It should be around here somewhere."

Consulting the compass duct-taped to my dash, I faced north and pointed to a gentle incline covered with a century's worth of pine growth. "It might be on the other side of that hill." Hunting for a graveyard abandoned over a hundred years ago is no easy task, especially if the township records suck.

Chesley hung my spare helmet over a handlebar and tucked his chin-length hair behind his ears. "The cemetery could be inside the thicket. The undergrowth's had plenty of time to cover the gravesites."

The June afternoon heated up, and I stripped off my helmet and jacket. "I hope not. I want to take photos of any inscriptions, count up the headstones, and call it done."

"How did Glory talk you into this? Seems odd she'd care about old burials."

"She thinks she's my boss. She assumed I'd do it on a

volunteer basis." I snorted. "As if." So, she offered me minimum wage. I refused, but made a fatal mistake. I said I'd need the rate the town was giving summer students. The Cranky Contessa screeched for a while and told me I was a bad citizen. Finally, she gave in and pointed me towards the municipal archives for maps. I hate her."

We crossed the road and ploughed through an expanse of waist-high grass. If the cemetery was inside the gloomy stand of trees, Chesley might come in handy, to serve as bear bait. I shoved him into the lead.

We skirted a couple of flowering shrubs with white, trumpet-shaped blossoms. I picked one and stuck it in my hair. Chesley stumbled and I fell on top of him. After that, I stayed back.

As interim mayor of Lockport, a town of 7,000 hardy souls on the shores of Lake Huron, Glory Yates was on a crazy power trip. Who cared if there were burial grounds being overtaken by time in the wilds of the township? Dust to dust, right? Not. She wanted them located, inventoried, photographed and restored. I'd do the first three, but Bliss Moonbeam Cornwall wasn't getting paid enough to restore anything. And, I'd run for mayor myself in the fall if that was the only way of preventing her from permanently slapping the gold chain of office around her neck. Although, someone was bound to strangle her with it five minutes into the first council meeting, so it was all good.

"You're earning some extra money, Bliss. Look at it that way."

We stopped to catch our breath at the edge of the forest. "Don't need another job." I gave him a nudge. "Let's do this."

Midday became twilight. The pines soared thirty feet

above our heads, spindly at first, then branching and tangling into a thick mass as the trees fought for sunlight.

"It's beautiful in here." Chesley turned his face up to the green ceiling and inhaled. "Don't you love the smell?"

"Yeah, awesome. But what's with all this ivy? How am I supposed to find graves? This doesn't look like a cemetery." The floor of a pine forest is usually spongy with fallen needles. Here, clumps of shiny, calf-high plants undulated as far as the eye could see, like emerald waves.

"That's not natural. Someone planted it." Chesley spoke with expert confidence.

I backed up. "I vote we strike this one off the list and not mention it to the Royal Pain."

Chesley dropped to his knees and burrowed into the ivy, giving me a tasteful view of his scrawny butt.

With a joyful hoot, he popped up. "Score. A *Piperia unalascensis*!" He pointed to a two-foot twig spiking out of the ground, half-entangled by the ivy. Trust a botanist to zero in on a stick.

"Super. I'm looking for tombstones."

"You might know it as a Slender Spire Orchid, Bliss."

"That's what I thought." Since Chesley and his mum, Ivy Belcourt, owned the greenhouse that employed me, he was technically one of my bosses. Still, I had no patience with his botanical enthusiasms and refused to encourage them.

"This genus is considered globally secure but very rare in this area. Did you know this plant grew from Alaska through Manitoulin Island to the east coast of Canada during the glacial melt 10,000 years ago?"

"Unbelievable." I scuffed through the undergrowth,

stopping when my boot connected with a hard object. Kicking aside the vegetation, I uncovered a grave marker. Green plant scum obscured the inscription.

I prepared to share the happy news with Chesley, but he pulled a miniature set of gardening implements out of his pocket and selected a trowel.

"What are you doing?"

"I'm taking this specimen back to the greenhouse."

"This could be crown land. Do you know the penalty for digging in crown land?"

He made a show of looking around. "So, who's going to tell? Anyway, the plant isn't endangered."

Fine. I searched for tombstones, finding another dozen. They had all been flattened by time and the elements, and inscriptions were mostly illegible. Without an army of volunteers, I couldn't see a way of enumerating the dead and restoring their final resting places.

Chesley stood beside a hillock of earth that rose several feet high, bare of greenery. "You should come and look at this, Bliss."

I trudged over and peered into — a hole. It was approximately six feet long and four wide on ground level but narrowed in toward the bottom. "So?"

"Look closer."

I inched toward the edge of the pit and saw rotted splinters of wood. Coffin pieces.

My pupils dilated to their maximum and the shards of wood mingled with rounded, lighter objects. My mind filled in the pattern. "Bones."

"Yup."

A thin shaft of sunlight pierced the overhead canopy, scattering cheerful rays across the heaps of earth under our feet.

Chesley balanced close to the edge. "Somebody dug this grave up by hand. You can still see the shovel marks."

"There's the tombstone." A weathered marker leaned against a tree trunk. I slithered down and tilted the stone to catch the light. The lettering was barely legible. "Catherine Mileski. She died at age 16 in 1847 and was the beloved wife of Stanley Mileski. Shit, the pioneers were a bunch of pedophiles."

"Didn't there used to be a Polish settlement nearby?"

I climbed up beside Chesley. "Guess we found it." I pulled a folded piece of paper from my pocket. "St. Stanislaus Cemetery."

When I shifted to put the paper away, my foot sank into loose soil and I fell to my knees. The earth collapsed beneath me. Chesley grabbed my sleeve, but the thin fabric ripped. I slipped and rolled over the edge.

My body slammed against the wood and bone fragments. Chesley's white face appeared above me, one hand holding the T-shirt, his grape-green eyes popping.

"Are you okay? Can you move?"

I flexed my legs. Check. Reaching my hands over my head, I touched tree roots spilling from the wall. Rolling over, I got to my hands and knees. "I think I see Elvis."

I remembered the bones and staggered to my feet. My ass hurt like you wouldn't believe and my spine shot forks of fire.

Chesley moved back as clumps of dirt fell onto my head. "Can you climb out?'

I extended my arms and dug my fingers into the sides of the grave. The earth crumbled. I worked my way around the hole with the same result.

"I'm stuck. We need help." I pulled my phone from the front pocket of my jeans. "I'm not getting a signal."

"Me either. I'll have to go back to the road. Shall I call Chief Redfern?"

"Just call 911 and mention my name. They know me." Mosquitoes buzzed around my head, preparing to land on my naked shoulders. "Toss my shirt down."

The crashing sounds as he ran to the road stopped abruptly. Surely the numbskull hadn't fallen into another grave? "Chesley! Can you hear me?"

"I found a second *Pipera unalascensis*. I'll dig it up so I don't lose track of it."

"I'm going to kick your ass when I get out of here."

"Have to seal the bag. There. You're practically rescued."

I tried not to think about my co-inhabitant's cause of death. When did I last have a tetanus shot? Oh, right. Last December, when I had been shot. The ER doctor got carried away and I was covered if a polio, diphtheria, or whooping cough outbreak hit town. But, not cholera or smallpox. Or plague.

My shirt had a long tear down the front. I put in on backwards so the rescuers wouldn't be distracted by my grave-besmirched lacy bra. A low moaning drifted through the tops of the pines. Just wind. The scurrying noises were squirrels running through the branches.

No doubt about it, I needed to rethink what I'd do, and not do, for money. First time out on the cemetery job, and it could be my last. If the botanic savant managed to summon help to get me out of this hole, I was going to take the cheap badge and the copy of the Cemetery Act that Glory had given me and shove them down her throat.

To pass the time, I used the screen light on my phone to scan the grave. I directed the light to the far side. And, back.

Bony fingers of ice squeezed my neck. Where was Catherine Mileski's head?

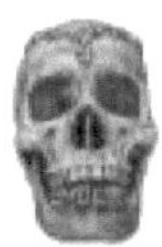

(NOTE: READ THE REST of Skull Garden to find out exactly what happened to Catherine's head. You won't believe it!)

REVIEWS

CORPSE FLOWER (Book 1, winner of Unhanged Arthur Award):

"What a delightful read! I polished it off in one sitting and immediately moved to book 2. The protagonist is a plucky, stubborn and slightly crass young woman. In spite of her poverty, she is honest, hardworking and kind to a fault. I haven't laughed that hard since Kathleen Hering's Designer Mystery series. It takes a talented author to bring the humour from a page to laugh out loud enjoyment and Ms Ferris joins the rare few at top of that class.

Adding to the story - a mouthy parrot. an Amorphophallus Titanum, a coywolf, wetlands that harbour spotted turtles, a gang of drug dealers and the towns new police chief, all of which in this cleverly woven plot will have you hooked and booked until you reach the end."

"A super and hilarious read! I discovered this author in my search for books that have won or been shortlisted for Arthur Ellis awards and am I ever glad that I did. I like to have a light and hopefully humorous book to read after finishing a more serious, gritty or violent crime novel by such authors as Rick Mofina or Don Easton among many others and this one sure fills that bill. I haven't had so many giggles and outright belly laughs since some of Renee Pawlish's early Reed Ferguson books or Mary Jane Maffini's Camilla MacPhee series and all the fun is combined with a pretty good crime story as well. I don't think there is any character in this book that isn't somewhat quirky and everyone of the plots and subplots are unique, hilarious and entertaining enough to make the book a good read. Bliss and Neil are both very likeable characters and I'm looking forward to more of their exploits when I need another good laugh with another good mystery. Simon is really something else! I had Snake all figured out as soon as he appeared but then I started doubting myself but it turned out I was right. I also had the Quigley's pegged, too, but then I started to question that as well and these points just illustrate what a well written mystery this is. I am definitely going to read the rest of this series and I'll have to read "Cheat The Hangman" as it was also shortlisted for the Unhanged Arthur. I've found a new author to add to my favourite Canadian authors list!"

SHROUD OF ROSES (Book 2)

"Award-winning author, Gloria Ferris, has written another delightful, humorous, murder mystery. Picking up where "Corpse Flower" left off, Bliss Moonbeam Cornwall will make you laugh out loud as she continues to meddle in police affairs, much to the frustration of her love interest, Lockport's chief of police, Neil Redfern. With a colourful cast of characters ranging from those introduced in her previous book to some suspicious types from "Dogtown", Ferris takes us on a hilarious journey complete with twists and turns to discover who was responsible for a murder at her high school 15 years earlier. When another former grad turns up dead, Bliss's life becomes complicated and dangerous. A completely entertaining read!"

"Shroud of Roses wastes no time as it quickly kicks into another great mystery. It is darker than Corpse Flower, but shares the same fun pacing and wit. There's more at stake for Bliss this time, as she begins digging into the string of murders, despite the police warning her about meddling. A great second book in the series - highly recommend!"

SKULL GARDEN "Book 3"

"Another great book in the Cornwall and Redfern series. I'm really hoping this isn't the last book though because I'm enjoying this series so much. This one is another great mystery with lots of subplots and humour integrated into it. The relationship between Bliss and Redfern has progressed a lot since book #1 so I want to see how their story ends as well. It can't possibly stop here so please write another one, Gloria Ferris! Lol."

"Another winner in the Cornwall and Redfern series. Loved every moment of it! Bliss Cornwall has a talent for involvement with the most off beat characters and situations. She taught me how NOT to use bear repellent, and to avoid jimsonweed. If you want the details you'll have to read Skull Garden for yourself. I hope another adventure (the wedding kind?) for these two likable characters won't be far behind."

WEDDED BLISS (Book 3.5, Novelette)

"Ferris has done it again! Fun read. Well, they are finally doing it! Bliss Moonbeam Cornwall and Neil Philip Redfern, known to each other as Cornwall and Redfern, are getting married today. The whole gang is there. Glory, the wedding planner for this wedding and mayor of Lockport, Pan, her live-in help, Cornwall's cousin Dougal with his very rude parrot, Simon and many more. . . . and that's not all -the exes, his and hers! Mayhem ensues. You can be sure that Cornwall and Redfern's marriage will as fun and as full of adventure as their courtship was. I can't wait."

"Spunky Bliss Moonbeam Cornwall of the "Cornwall & Redfern Mystery Series" (Corpse Flower, Shroud of Roses, and Skull Garden) stays true to her quirky self, even on her wedding day. Bliss and her handsome Police Chief fiancé Neil Redfern's nuptials are a roller-coaster ride of "fishy" mishaps and crimes, made light by Ferris's cheeky sense of humour. Interesting and eccentric characters from the previous books attend this unconventional wedding. Even a foul-mouthed parrot makes an appearance. Without giving away the details, let's just say nothing can get in the way of Cornwall and Redfern's love for each other and their determination to tie the knot."

DARK BLOSSOMING (Book 4)

"Have always enjoyed Gloria Ferris Books but especially her Cornwall and Redfern Series. Always interesting with twists and turns of each storyline. And the personalities involved and relationships. Keep them coming. Always room for more Cornwall and Redfern."

Don't miss out!

Visit the website below and you can sign up to receive emails whenever Gloria Ferris publishes a new book. There's no charge and no obligation.

https://books2read.com/r/B-A-FVUE-FMKNC

BOOKS 2 READ

Connecting independent readers to independent writers.